FORGOTTEN HER

SEEKING THE LOST

PRIYA V NAIR

Contents

Foreword

Dear Reader,

"It's a rare honor to witness an artist's growth and an even greater privilege to be a part of it. As I write this, I'm filled with pride and admiration for my dear friend, the author of this extraordinary book. Already the creator of two captivating works, she continues to redefine storytelling, offering readers fresh, introspective perspectives. Her latest book is no exception.

Forgotten Her is more than a story, it's a powerful ode to resilience, a journey through pain and healing, and a testament to the strength of the human spirit. Within these pages lies the untold path of those who have faced profound trauma and chosen to rise above it with courage and determination.

As her friend and editor, I have witnessed the raw vulnerability and unwavering dedication she poured into this work. Every page reflects her honesty, bravery, and commitment to shedding light on these deeply human experiences.

This book poignantly reminds us that healing isn't a single destination; it's an ongoing journey filled with setbacks, growth, and moments of light. Hope exists even in our darkest times, and Forgotten Her is a light for those who need it most.

I am certain this book will resonate deeply with readers, offering comfort, understanding, and inspiration. It's been an honor to be part of its creation, and I'm proud to stand with the author in sharing this profound work with the world."

—Lithin Thampy

Preface

Forgotten Her is a story of healing, struggle, and strength that lies within us, even in the most broken of moments. At its heart, the narrative follows Shraddha, a woman who has faced deep emotional scars and, through her own journey of recovery, has learned to heal not only herself but others around her. It is also the story of Maya, a woman caught in the tangled web of trauma, trying to find her way out, with Shraddha's quiet guidance helping her to begin the path of recovery.

This book is not just about the lives of Shraddha and Maya; it reflects the journeys of many who have faced pain and yet continue to fight for hope, strength, and peace. Forgotten Her aims to shed light on those stories that often remain in the shadows; stories of trauma, resilience, and eventual healing. It is a tribute to those who have suffered, who have struggled in silence, and those who are still finding their way.

To all those who feel forgotten, lost, or invisible, this book is for you. Your pain is seen, your struggles are real, and your healing is important. This story, though fictional, is a mirror to the lives of many, reminding us that we are never truly alone in our journeys.

May Shraddha and Maya's stories offer a flicker of hope to those still searching for their light, and may we all continue to support and uplift each other on this path of healing and self-discovery.

Acknowledgements

I would like to thank everyone who has supported me throughout this journey, especially my editor, friends, and family. Your encouragement and belief in me have made this book possible.

To the women whose stories of strength and resilience inspired "Forgotten Her," this book is for you.

Prologue

There are stories that stay hidden, not because they are forgotten, but because they are too painful to face. Shraddha knew this all too well. She had lived in the shadows of her own past, learning to survive, but never truly heal. Then, at Ashraya, something began to shift.

In the quiet moments of helping others, Shraddha realized that healing wasn't just about fixing what was broken. It was about learning to live again. But healing is never simple, and the journey is never easy.

Maya, broken in ways Shraddha could recognize all too well, came to Ashraya looking for a way to escape her pain. Little did they know, their paths were meant to cross. Together, they would learn that healing isn't about forgetting—it's about finding strength in the most unexpected places.

This is the story of two women who learned to rediscover their voices. It is for every woman who has ever felt lost, silenced, or invisible.

FRAGMENTED

> *"The soft, melodic tunes played gently in the background as the inmates entered the counseling room of Ashraya, a well-known psychiatric rehabilitation center on the outskirts of Vagamon. On a quiet hill away from the city's chaos, Ashraya became a place of solace. More than a space for healing, it was a refuge where many came to take a break from life."*

Shraddha grunted upon seeing the therapist, who greeted them with a smile that seemed forced. Mrs. Sheela had earned a bad reputation among the inmates due to her perceived insincerity and the unsolicited advice she often offered to those who simply wanted someone to listen.

Shraddha moved forward and took a seat as Sheela began her usual vague talk, "Life is a beautiful journey; ups and downs are just part of it... we don't need to care about what others think along the way."

"Here we go again! This lady, who dresses up like a supermodel for every session, is telling us not to care about others? The irony is just too much," Shraddha thought, smirking.

It had been three years since Shraddha arrived at the facility. By now, it felt more like home, and she knew every nook and cranny of the place. They called it "Ashraya," but the sense of shelter and comfort implied by the name seemed to exist only in words, not in reality.

As the session dragged on, Shraddha let her mind drift. Mrs. Sheela's words floated around the room, but they barely registered. Shraddha's eyes scanned the faces of the others, some listening intently, others with expressions as blank as hers. She had learned to read them, the subtle shifts in their eyes, the way their hands gripped the edges of their chairs. It was a language only those who'd spent time here could understand.

"Shraddha," Mrs. Sheela's voice cut through her thoughts, bringing her back to the present. "What do you think about what I said?"

She blinked, caught off guard. "About... not caring what others think?"

"Yes," Mrs. Sheela said, her smile stretching wider. "Isn't it a freeing concept?"

Shraddha hesitated, her mind racing for a response that wouldn't lead to another lecture. "I don't know", she said, looking away "Maybe for some people."

As Mrs. Sheela moved on to the next person, Shraddha's thoughts began to drift, slipping into that familiar, uncomfortable space she tried to avoid. The soft, melodic tunes in the room mingled with distant echoes of another time, another place...sounds she had worked so hard to drown out. She could feel her chest tightening, a slight tremor running through her hands, but she clenched her fingers into fists, grounding herself.

It had been three years since she found herself at "Ashraya." Three years of trying to piece together a sense of normalcy that always seemed just out of reach. There were moments when she could almost forget...when the world around her felt ordinary, and she could breathe without the shadow of the past creeping in. But then there were days, like today, when the weight of it all pressed down, heavy and suffocating.

Shraddha glanced around the room, her gaze flitting over the others. Some faces were familiar, stamped with lines of weariness and resignation. She knew their stories, or at least parts of them, just as they knew hers or rather, the version she allowed them to see. No one here ever talked about why they were at Ashraya, not really. It was as if speaking it aloud would give the past too much power, dragging it out of the dark corners where it lurked, waiting to pull it under.

The truth was, there were parts of her past she had buried so deep that she barely recognized them as her own anymore. Memories that flickered at the edge of her consciousness, threatening to surface whenever she let her guard down. They came to her in fragments; an unexpected scent, a whispered word, the way the light fell across a room...tiny, harmless things that could loosen her if she wasn't careful. So, she had learned to keep them locked away, hidden behind a wall of indifference, and practiced smiles.

Shraddha's focus wavered as she stared at the corner of the room, where a small potted plant sat on a dusty windowsill. It was barely thriving, its leaves yellowed and drooping. She had never paid much attention to it before, but today, something about its fragility caught her eye. It was as if it was clinging to life despite being forgotten, left to survive on its own. She wondered if that's how she appeared to others...fading, yet stubbornly hanging on.

As the session continued, Mrs. Sheela's words blurred into background noise, merging with the faint hum of the air conditioner. The room felt stifling, and Shraddha could sense a dull ache building at the back of her head. She rubbed her temples, trying to push away the discomfort, but it only seemed to grow stronger, like a tide rising inside her.

Then, a sudden noise, a chair scraping across the floor...jolted her back to the present. Her breath hitched, and for a brief moment, she felt as if the walls were closing in, squeezing the air out of her lungs. She glanced around, but no one else seemed to notice. To them, it was just an ordinary sound, but to her, it was a reminder of what, she didn't know. All she knew was that it made her feel exposed, as if a crack had opened up, letting something dark and unwelcome seep through.

"Shraddha?" Mrs. Sheela's voice was softer now, almost gentle. "Is everything alright?"

Shraddha forced a smile, though it felt more like a grimace. "Yeah, I'm fine." She didn't know if she was trying to convince Mrs. Sheela or herself. "Just... lost in thought."

Mrs. Sheela nodded, her eyes lingering on Shraddha for a moment longer than usual before she returned to addressing the group. Shraddha's shoulders relaxed slightly, relieved that the attention had shifted away from her. But even as she listened to the others speak, she could feel it, the restlessness beneath the surface, stirring and coiling like a serpent.

She hated this part of the day, the forced intimacy of group sessions, where everyone pretended to bare their souls while keeping the most important parts hidden. It was a strange kind of performance, a dance around their shared pain without ever touching it. Sometimes, she wondered if they were all just ghosts, drifting through their days without really existing.

The session ended with the usual platitudes, and the inmates began to file out of the room. Shraddha lingered for a moment, watching them go. Some walked quickly, eager to escape, while others moved slowly, as if reluctant to leave the safety of the room. She wondered where they went when they weren't here, what they did to pass the time. Did they, like her, wander the corridors of Ashraya, searching for something they couldn't name?

As she stood to leave, Shraddha felt a light touch on her arm. She turned to see another inmate, Rani, a middle-aged woman with kind eyes and a quiet demeanor. Rani rarely spoke during the sessions, but she had a way of observing things, of seeing people without them realizing it.

"You okay?" Rani asked softly, her brow furrowed with concern.

"Yeah, I'm fine," Shraddha said, repeating the lie that had become second nature to her. She offered a smile, hoping it would be enough to end the conversation.

Rani hesitated, as if she wanted to say more, but then she simply nodded and stepped back. "Take care," she said before walking away.

Shraddha watched her go, feeling a pang of guilt for brushing off someone who had only been trying to help. But she couldn't explain it...not to Rani, not to Mrs. Sheela, not to anyone. How could she put into words the things she herself didn't fully understand? The feelings that twisted inside her, dark and tangled, like roots burrowing deep beneath the surface.

With a sigh, she left the counseling room and made her way down the long, narrow hallway that led to her dormitory. The lights flickered overhead, casting dim, uneven shadows on the floor. It was late afternoon, but the sky outside was overcast, making everything feel dull and muted. She could hear the faint murmur of voices from other rooms, the occasional clatter of footsteps echoing through the corridors.

As she reached her room, Shraddha paused for a moment before opening the door, her hand resting on the handle. For a second, she felt the familiar urge to turn around and keep walking, to go anywhere but inside. But she pushed it down, forcing herself to step over the threshold.

The room was small, with bare walls and a single bed pushed up against one side. A thin curtain hung over the window, fluttering slightly in the breeze. There were no personal touches, no photographs or trinkets to make the space feel like hers. It was as if she was afraid to leave a mark, to make herself known in a place where she wasn't sure she belonged.

Her eyes turned towards a small box, almost hidden from view. She had placed it there intentionally, tucking it out of reach and out of sight. That box held the memories she wasn't yet ready to confront, a part of her past she wasn't prepared to face. She had buried it here, as if hoping that by keeping it locked away, she could keep her memories...and the pain they carried; just as contained.

Shraddha sank onto the bed, her body heavy with exhaustion. She closed her eyes, letting the silence envelop her. But even in the quiet, she couldn't escape the echoes...the sounds that haunted her, the whispers of a past that refused to stay buried. She thought about the others at Ashraya, about how they all carried their own burdens, invisible but ever-present. And she wondered if they, too, felt this way....caught in an uncertainity between remembering and forgetting, struggling to find a place where they could finally rest.

In the stillness, a faint memory flickered to life, like a match struck in the dark. She could almost see it; vague and blurred, just out of reach. The more she tried to grasp it, the more it slipped away, leaving behind a hollow ache that lingered long after the image had faded.

Shraddha opened her eyes, staring up at the ceiling. She knew she couldn't keep running from it forever. Whatever it was, it was waiting for her, biding its time. And one day, she would have to face it. But not today. Not yet.

CHAPTER TWO

TIDES

The next morning arrived with a light drizzle, the kind that made everything appear softer, muted, as if the world was caught in a eternal sigh. Shraddha awoke to the gentle patter of rain against her window, a sound that had always brought her a strange comfort. It reminded her of home, though she no longer knew where that was or what it meant.

As she got ready, she caught her reflection in the small, cracked mirror hanging on the wall. Her eyes looked dull, dark circles faintly shadowing beneath them. She touched her face, tracing the faint lines that had begun to etch themselves around her mouth, wondering when she had started to look so tired.

Breakfast was a quiet affair, as it always was at Ashraya. The dining hall buzzed with the low murmur of voices, the music of clinking utensils and muted conversations. Shraddha took her usual spot at the corner table, away from the clusters of people who gathered in small groups. She liked it this way...observing, but never part of it.

Across the room, she spotted Rani sitting with a few others, her face lit up in a rare smile. Shraddha felt a sting of something; guilt, perhaps, or maybe just a longing she didn't quite understand. Rani had always tried to reach out, to connect, but Shraddha kept pulling back, retreating into her shell. It was easier that way. Safer.

She was halfway through her meal when the door to the dining hall creaked open, and a woman she hadn't seen before walked in. She was young, in her mid-twenties, with sharp features and a gaze that seemed to pierce through the room, scanning everything with an unsettling intensity. Her clothes were simple, but there was an air of insolence about her, as if she was daring anyone to judge her.

For a moment, their eyes met, and Shraddha quickly looked away, feeling exposed under the weight of the stranger's stare. But she couldn't resist glancing back, curiosity gnawing at her. The woman took a seat at an empty table, her posture rigid, as though bracing herself for something.

The rest of the day passed in a blur of routine; chores, group activities, and a few moments of letup in the courtyard when the rain subsided. Shraddha found herself thinking about the new arrival, wondering what had brought her here and what story she carried within her. Ashraya was full of stories, each one more complex and tragic than the next, but they all shared a common thread: the desire to escape, to find solace from whatever had driven them to seek refuge within these walls.

That afternoon, Shraddha was surprised to find herself called into Mrs. Sheela's office. She couldn't recall doing anything that might warrant a private session, but she went anyway, her curiosity outweighing her apprehension.

Mrs. Sheela was seated behind her desk, her expression calm and composed, she was dressed in a sleek, fitted blazer over a bright floral blouse, her hair perfectly styled, and a hint of gloss shining on her lips. It was as if she had just stepped out of a magazine cover, a stark contrast to the understated surroundings of Ashraya, but Shraddha could sense a shift in her manner, a subtle tension that hadn't been there before.

"Please, have a seat," Mrs. Sheela said, gesturing to the chair opposite her.

Shraddha hesitated for a moment before sitting down, her eyes flicking to the stack of papers on the desk, neatly arranged in a way that seemed almost too deliberate.

"I wanted to talk to you about something," Mrs. Sheela began, her tone careful, measured. "There's a new person who has just arrived at Ashraya. Her name is Maya. I believe you might have seen her in the dining hall this morning."

Shraddha nodded, a little taken aback by the fact that Mrs. Sheela had noticed her noticing Maya. "Yes, I saw her," she said. "Why are you telling me this?"

"She's going through a difficult time," Mrs. Sheela continued, ignoring the question. "It's her first day here, and I think it would help if she had someone to talk to, someone who understands what it's like to be... new to this place."

Shraddha felt a flicker of annoyance. "And you think I'm the best person for that?" she asked, unable to keep the edge out of her voice.

"I think you understand more than most," Mrs. Sheela said, meeting her gaze. "You've been here for three years, Shraddha. You know what it's like to feel lost, to struggle with finding your place. I'm not asking you to become her best friend. Just... make her feel a little less alone."

The words pricked, not because they were untrue, but because they were. She didn't want to be reminded of how long she had been at Ashraya, of how she still hadn't figured out where she belonged. But she could see the plea in Mrs. Sheela's eyes, and for reasons she couldn't quite explain, she found herself nodding.

"Alright," she said quietly. "I'll try."

Later that evening, Shraddha found herself back in the courtyard, the air cool and damp after the rain. She spotted Maya sitting on a bench under the shade of a large banyan tree, her head bent low, hands fidgeting in her lap. For a moment, Shraddha thought about turning around, and retreating to her room. But then she remembered the look on Mrs. Sheela's face, and before she could change her mind, she made her way over.

"Hey," she said, stopping a few feet away. "Mind if I sit here?"

Maya glanced up, her eyes wary, but she nodded. "Sure."

They sat in silence for a few minutes, the sound of the leaves rustling overhead filling the gaps between them. Shraddha didn't know what to say, how to start a conversation with someone she barely knew. But she also knew what it felt like to be new, to have a thousand thoughts swirling in your head with no one to share them with.

"It's kind of overwhelming, isn't it?" she said finally, her voice soft. "Coming here, I mean."

Maya's lips twitched into a faint smile. "That obvious, huh?"

"A little," Shraddha admitted, smiling back. "I've been here a while, so I kind of know how it feels. But it gets easier... eventually."

"Does it?" Maya asked, her voice barely more than a whisper. "Because right now, it feels like I'm never going to get used to this."

Shraddha hesitated, unsure how to respond. She wanted to offer comfort, to say that everything would be okay, but she also knew that it would be a lie. And if there was one thing she had learned at Ashraya, it was that lies, no matter how well intentioned, had a way of making things worse.

"It takes time," she said finally. "More time than you'd think. But you're not alone in this. We're all trying to figure it out, in our own way."

Maya looked at her, and for the first time, Shraddha saw something in her eyes...a flicker of hope, or maybe just a momentary respite from the weight she was carrying.

"Thank you," she said, her voice barely audible.

Shraddha nodded, and as they sat there, the night creeping in around them, she felt something shift inside her. It wasn't a resolution, not exactly, but a sense of understanding, a quiet acceptance that maybe, just maybe, there was a way forward, even if it was slow and uncertain.

The next few days passed with a tentative rhythm. Shraddha and Maya continued to cross paths in the courtyard, at mealtimes, and during the group activities at Ashraya. Each time, Shraddha made an effort to reach out, small gestures, brief exchanges, but always careful not to push too hard. And Maya responded, though her responses were often guarded, as if she were still testing the waters, deciding whether to trust this unexpected overture of friendship.

One afternoon, as they sat on opposite ends of a bench in the courtyard, the conversation stalled, the silence stretching longer than usual. Maya seemed lost in thought, her eyes distant, and Shraddha wondered if she should say something or just let it be. Before she could decide, Maya suddenly spoke, her voice breaking the stillness.

"You know, I thought it would be easier to just... disappear when I came here," she said, her tone flat, almost detached. "But it's like everything follows you, no matter where you go."

Shraddha didn't know how to respond, so she just nodded, hoping that her silence would be enough to encourage Maya to keep talking. But instead, Maya got up, muttering something about needing to be alone, and walked away, leaving Shraddha feeling as if she had somehow failed. She watched as Maya disappeared down the hall, a familiar sense of helplessness settling over her.

The following day, Shraddha found herself being called into Mrs. Sheela's office again. She entered with a mixture of apprehension and resignation, unsure what to expect this time.

Mrs. Sheela was dressed in her usual sharp attire—a tailored, deep emerald green dress that accentuated her tall, graceful frame. Her hair was styled neatly, her eyes framed with a subtle touch of eyeliner. She looked up from her paperwork as Shraddha entered, her expression not quite as warm as before.

"I've noticed things haven't been easy with Maya," Mrs. Sheela said, getting straight to the point. "She's been avoiding group activities and hasn't spoken much to anyone. I understand why you might be finding it difficult, but I thought you might be able to reach her."

Shraddha stiffened, feeling the sting of the implied reprimand. "I've tried," she said, struggling to keep her voice steady. "But she's... it's not easy. She doesn't want to talk, and I didn't want to force her."

Mrs. Sheela's gaze softened, a hint of empathy seeping through her usual composed demeanor. "I know, Shraddha. I see how hard it can be. But maybe that's why I thought you could help her. You've been in a similar place, feeling lost, trying to find your footing. I'm not asking you to carry her burden. Just... let her know she's not alone in it. Sometimes, when you're struggling, it can help to see that someone else understands."

Shraddha hesitated, her frustration and guilt mingling. "I'm not sure I'm the right person," she admitted, her voice barely above a whisper. "I don't even have my own life figured out."

"I'm not asking you to fix her problems, or yours," Mrs. Sheela said, leaning back in her chair. "Just to be there, to listen if she needs it. If she pushes you away, that's fine. But sometimes, simply knowing someone's willing to try can make a difference."

Shraddha left the office feeling deflated, her mind replaying the conversation over and over. Had she been holding back? Maybe Mrs. Sheela was right. Maybe she had been too afraid of saying the wrong thing, of overstepping, and in the process, she may heal as well.

For the next three days, Shraddha didn't see Maya at all. She asked around, but no one seemed to know where she was. The absence gnawed at her, a quiet worry that she couldn't shake off. Yet, she hesitated to approach Mrs. Sheela, replaying their last conversation in her mind, feeling as if she'd already failed.

On the fourth day, she found herself sitting in the courtyard once more, staring blankly at the swaying branches of the banyan tree. She was so lost in her thoughts that she didn't notice Maya approaching until she was standing right in front of her.

"Hey," Maya said, her voice soft, almost hesitant. "Can I sit?"

Shraddha looked up, her heart leaping with a mix of surprise and relief. "Of course."

They sat in silence for a few moments, the air heavy with unspoken words. Finally, it was Maya who spoke.

"I'm sorry I've been avoiding you," she said, her words spilling out quickly, as if afraid she might lose her nerve. "I just... didn't know how to handle everything. And then I heard what Mrs. Sheela said to you, and I felt like I was just making things harder for everyone."

Shraddha's heart sank, a pain of guilt and sadness washing over her. So, Maya had known. "It's okay," she said, her voice gentle. "You don't have to apologize. I should have tried harder to be there for you."

"No," Maya interrupted, shaking her head, her voice growing firmer. "You were the only one who actually tried. And I... I just ran away." She paused, glancing down at her hands, fingers nervously twisting together. "I guess I'm not used to people being kind without expecting something in return."

Shraddha felt a lump in her throat, unsure how to respond. Instead, she reached out, gently covering Maya's hand with her own. "You don't have to explain yourself to me," she said quietly. "I'm here. Whenever you're ready, I'm here."

For a moment, it seemed like Maya might pull away, her gaze flickering with uncertainty. But then she sighed, her shoulders slumping as if she were finally allowing herself to relax. "I want to try," she said, her voice barely more than a whisper. "But I don't know how."

Shraddha squeezed her hand, offering a small, tentative smile. "We'll figure it out," she said softly.

CHAPTER THREE

UNSPOKEN

The air at Ashraya had shifted, and for the first time since arriving, Shraddha felt a glimmer of happiness. Days passed in a gentle rhythm, punctuated by laughter and shared experiences with Maya. They explored the sprawling gardens together, their conversations growing deeper as they painted their hopes onto canvases, each stroke symbolizing their budding friendship.

One afternoon, they discovered a secluded corner of the garden where wildflowers bloomed freely. It became their sanctuary, a place to share secrets and dreams. Shraddha cherished these moments, feeling as though they were building something beautiful together—an unspoken pact of understanding and support.

"Do you think we'll always be here?" Maya asked one day, twirling a flower in her fingers.

Shraddha smiled; her heart warm. "I hope so. We can create our own little world if we want."

But as the days turned into weeks, Shraddha began to sense an undercurrent of tension. Maya, who had once embraced their shared joy, started to withdraw at times, her laughter replaced with silence. Shraddha felt a growing sense of urgency; she wanted to help Maya feel safe and supported, but she also feared overstepping her boundaries.

One day, while sitting in their secret garden, Maya's demeanour shifted. The laughter faded, replaced by a heaviness that hung in the air. Shraddha tried to lighten the mood. "What if we planted some flowers here? It would make it even more beautiful!"

Maya looked at her, the light in her eyes dimming. "Maybe it's too late for me to bloom," she said quietly.

Shraddha's heart sank. "You're not too late for anything. We can grow together, you know?"

Maya nodded but didn't reply, and the silence stretched uncomfortably. Shraddha felt a knot of worry tighten in her stomach.

As they continued to spend time together, Shraddha's feelings of responsibility for Maya grew. She no longer saw this as just Mrs. Sheela's assignment; it had transformed into a deep, personal commitment. She was invested in Maya's well-being, wanting to be the friend Maya needed.

Yet, beneath that sense of duty was an unsettling awareness. Shraddha could feel the weight of Maya's past creeping into their moments of joy. She was acutely aware of the pain that lay just below the surface, threatening to disrupt their fragile bond.

One evening, as they shared a simple dinner in the dining hall, the atmosphere was warm, filled with the low murmur of conversation and the clinking of plates. Shraddha felt a sense of contentment wash over her as they exchanged playful banter. Suddenly, the calmness was shattered when a fellow resident rushed in, her face pale with urgency.

"Maya!" the girl exclaimed, her voice rising above the din. "I overheard something about you... something terrible. Is it true that you were raped?"

The room fell silent, the words hanging heavily in the air like a dark cloud. Shraddha's heart raced, her pulse pounding in her ears. She glanced at Maya, whose face drained of colour, eyes wide with shock and humiliation.

"How did you feel to be there?" the girl pressed; her curiosity unaware to the pain she was inflicting. "What was it like?"

In that moment, everything changed. Maya's expression shifted from shock to a tight mask of anguish. Shraddha reached out, wanting to comfort her, to offer support, but Maya seemed to retreat within herself, shrinking back from the spotlight that had suddenly fallen on her.

The room buzzed with whispers, glances tearing between Maya and the newcomer, who seemed entirely unaware of the havoc she had unleashed. Shraddha felt a mix of anger and despair. How could someone be so thoughtless?

"Maya, let's go," Shraddha urged softly, her heart aching at the distress evident on Maya's face.

But Maya shook her head, her eyes brimming with unshed tears. "Just... leave me alone," she whispered, her voice cracking under the weight of her pain.

As Shraddha stood, feeling helpless and frustrated, she watched Maya's walls slam shut, locking away the light they had begun to share. After dinner, Maya vanished, retreating to her room, leaving Shraddha alone in a whirlpool of confusion and concern.

Days turned into a haze of worry. Maya began to isolate herself again, avoiding Shraddha, group activities, and even meals. The joy that had briefly illuminated their friendship flashed and dimmed, leaving Shraddha in misery, unable to understand what had gone wrong.

The next day brought unexpected news. Shraddha overheard a group of women whispering in the hallway, their voices low and filled with concern. As she approached, she caught snippets of their conversation.

"I heard she tried to harm herself," one woman said. "I can't believe it… how could someone let it get that far?"

Shraddha's heart dropped. The words felt like a punch to her gut, and she stumbled back, struggling to process what she had just heard. Maya had been in such a dark place that it had led her to consider ending it all. She ran back to her room feeling helpless, lost…

She a sat on the edge of her bed, the evening light streaming through the curtains and casting soft shadows on the walls. The walls were decorated with colourful drawings and photographs, each representing happy moments—birthdays, celebrations, and smiles that felt like distant memories now. But today, everything seemed dull and grey, overshadowed by a heavy cloud of thoughts that hung over her.

The events of the past few days rushed through her mind, especially the hurtful question from dinner: "How did you feel to be there?" It echoed in her thoughts like a sad song, pulling at her heart. It had broken the fragile wall Maya had built around her pain, exposing the deep hurt she had been trying so hard to hide.

As Shraddha lay back on her bed, staring at the ceiling, she felt a familiar comfort turning strange, almost suffocating.

She couldn't help but think back to her own childhood—a time when innocence was delicate and easily shattered. She remembered a Christmas vacation when she was eight years old, filled with laughter and festive cheer. The house was alive with twinkling lights, and the sweet smell of freshly baked cookies filled the air, mixing with the soft sound of carols. She had been so excited, filled with the magic of the season, blissfully unaware that her happiness would soon be overshadowed by a terrible event.

That particular evening began like any other. Shraddha wore her favourite red dress, the one with the lacy edge that made her feel like a princess. Her mother braided her hair, and her father lifted her up to place a star on top of the Christmas tree—a moment that felt truly magical. It was indeed a beautiful day for them, they shared stories, played games, and enjoyed a delicious feast her mother had prepared especially for her favourite, "Chicken Hariyali".

"Mumma, I love you so much, you made my favourite today" little Shraddha hugged her mom tightly. Her mom smiled warmly and pecked a kiss on her cheek. "Anything for my princess," she whispered, smoothing down Shraddha's hair.

That evening appeared to be beautiful and surrounded by the warmth of her family, she thought their happiness would last forever.

Everything felt just right until her aunt, her dad's elder sister; arrived unexpectedly, accompanied by her son, Shraddha's favourite cousin. Little Shraddha's face lit up with joy. "Anup bhaiya!" she exclaimed. He gifted her a Barbie doll she had been dreaming about for months, and she couldn't contain her excitement. As a single child, she looked up to him as the older brother she never had, a constant source of joy and companionship. Every time he visited, it felt like the world had more colors, more games to play, and more laughter to share.

However, that night, things changed. The adults gathered in the living room, their laughter and chatter muffled by the walls, leaving the children to entertain themselves. Shraddha's cousin leaned in closer, his familiar mischievous grin playing on his lips. "Let's go play outside," he said, his eyes sparkling with excitement. Shraddha's heart skipped with joy, thinking it was yet another of their secret little adventures. She grabbed his hand, her tiny fingers wrapping around his, blissfully unaware of the storm that was about to shatter her perfect world.

She followed him into the cold night, the world transformed into a winter wonderland. The snow crunched under their feet, and she felt a thrill as she chased him into the shadows, her breath forming little clouds in the crisp air. The night was filled with distant laughter, but little did she know that those sounds would soon be drowned out by her own fear.

As they stepped away from the house, her cousin's mood shifted; his playful tone turned darker. He led her to a hidden spot behind the garage, far from the warmth and laughter of the gathering. In her innocent mind, it felt like a secret adventure. But the moment he pushed her against the cold wall, everything changed.

His hands, which once held hers with warmth, now gripped her shoulders tightly, pinning her in place. The playful sparkle in his eyes had vanished, replaced by a look that frightened her. Shraddha's heart began to pound, and a wave of confusion washed over her as she tried to understand what was happening. This wasn't the game she had expected; this was something far more sinister.

"Let's play a different kind of game," he whispered, his voice no longer gentle. Shraddha's small, innocent mind struggled to make sense of his words, but the coldness in his tone made her stomach twist with unease. Her breath hitched, a knot forming in her throat, and she tried to step back, but he was stronger.

Fear started to seep in as she looked up at him, searching for the cousin she knew—the one who always protected her, who made her laugh. But there was no trace of him in the dark, menacing figure that now loomed over her. "I...I don't want to play anymore...you are hurting me bhaiya," she stammered, her voice trembling, barely audible.

He ignored her words, his grip tightening. Panic began to rise within her, and she struggled to pull away, but it only made him press harder. "Stop moving," he hissed, and the sharpness of his voice made her freeze. Her mind screamed at her to run, to cry out for help, but she was paralyzed by a fear she had never known.

The night around them was still, the distant hum of carols from the house mingling with the rustle of the wind. To the world, it was just another cold December night, but for Shraddha, it marked the beginning of a nightmare she couldn't escape. She felt the cold seeping through her dress, the roughness of the wall against her back, and the suffocating sensation of being trapped.

Tears welled up in her eyes as she realized there was no escape, and the warmth that had filled her heart just moments ago was replaced by a chilling dread. She wanted to scream, but no sound came out; her voice was locked behind a wall of fear. As the moments dragged on, her cousin's touch grew harsher, and the reality of what was happening began to sink in.

Shraddha's world shattered in that instant. Her childhood, once bright and full of joy, was suddenly eclipsed by a darkness she couldn't understand. She felt her spirit break, piece by piece, as she was forced to endure a reality no child should ever face. The lights from the house, which once seemed so welcoming, now felt like a distant, unreachable comfort, and she realized with horror how alone she truly was.

The night dragged on, each second stretching into an eternity. Shraddha's mind retreated into itself, trying to find a safe place to hide from the pain, from the fear, from the betrayal. She clung to the memory of the Christmas star her father had lifted her to place atop the tree, a moment of magic that felt like it belonged to another world. But even that memory was slowly being swallowed by the darkness, leaving her with nothing but an aching emptiness.

When it was finally over, her cousin stepped back, his expression unreadable. Shraddha crumpled to the ground, her body shaking, her heart shattered. She didn't understand why this had happened, why someone she trusted had hurt her in ways she couldn't even begin to comprehend. She wanted to ask him why, but the words never came. All she could do was lie there, the snow around her dampened by her tears, as the weight of what had been taken from her pressed down on her small, fragile frame.

Her cousin knelt beside her, his tone creepily calm as he said, "Don't tell anyone, okay? This is our secret. Even if you tell, they won't believe you, and it'll only you cause trouble." His words were a cruel mockery of the bond they once shared, and Shraddha felt a new wave of fear crash over her. She didn't want to keep this secret, but the threat in his voice silenced her.

The sound of approaching footsteps made him quickly stand up, and he gave her one last, chilling look before turning back toward the house. As he disappeared into the light, Shraddha was left alone in the dark, the cold seeping through to her bones. She pulled her knees up to her chest, hugging herself tightly, as if trying to hold together the pieces of herself that had been shattered.

The distant sound of laughter from the house drifted over to her, a cruel reminder of the warmth and safety she could no longer reach. She didn't know how long she sat there, numb and broken, before she finally found the strength to stand and slowly make her way back inside.

But the experience haunted her, leaving a shadow over her childhood, filling her with feelings of betrayal and loneliness that she couldn't shake off.

As she lay on her bed, tears streamed down her cheeks. For the first time in years, she felt the weight of that trauma pressing down on her chest. It was as if all the emotions she had bottled up were finally demanding to be felt. She wrestled with the question that loomed over her: how could she support Maya when she hadn't faced her own pain?

As the tears continued to flow, Shraddha felt a sense of relief mingled with the deep ache in her heart. She had tried so hard to suppress her feelings, to bury them beneath layers of forced smiles and cheerful conversations. The thought of sharing her pain with anyone had always felt like an impossible challenge.

She recalled the one time she had dared to voice her torment to her parents. It had been a fragile moment, one she had approached with trembling hands and a heart full of hope. Sitting at the kitchen table, she had summoned all her courage and whispered her fears about her cousin.

"Mom, Dad, something happened that night… something I can't forget," she had begun, her voice barely above a whisper.

But their reactions had shattered her. Instead of the comfort she had desperately sought, her father had looked at her with alarm, and her mother's face had filled with worry. "Shraddha, we can't ruin the relationship with your cousin's family. They've been part of our lives for so long," her mother had said, her voice strained. "You must learn to forget and move on. It's just a misunderstanding."

Their dismissive response had struck her like a thunderclap. She had watched as their eyes shifted away from her, their discomfort palpable. In that moment, her heart had felt like it was breaking. The very people she had trusted to understand her pain had urged her to silence it.

Shraddha felt the weight of their words crushing her spirit once more. The fear of damaging familial bonds had bound her in chains of silence, and she had learned to wear her mask even tighter. She had been left to grapple with her trauma alone, her cries muffled beneath a veneer of normalcy. The echo of that conversation haunted her, reinforcing the notion that vulnerability was a weakness, a threat to the delicate fabric of family ties.

Days turned into months, and the trauma that she had pushed aside began to manifest in other ways…anxiety, nightmares, and an overwhelming sense of loneliness. She had tried to act like everything was fine, but the mask she wore became increasingly difficult to maintain. Eventually, the pain became too great to bear in silence which brought her to this place three years ago…Ashrya

As she lay there, lost in the swirl of memories, a soft knock on the door broke through her thoughts. Startled, Shraddha sat up, quickly wiping the tears from her cheeks. For a moment, she hesitated, her heart still heavy with the weight of her past, as if the knock had awakened her from a dark, endless dream.

Another gentle tap followed, more insistent yet patient, urging her to respond. She took a shaky breath, trying to compose herself. Whoever it was, they had unknowingly pulled her back from the painful depths she had been drowning in, forcing her to face the present once more.

CHAPTER FOUR

ACHE

The soft knock echoed in her mind, pulling her from the depths of her thoughts. She stood up, her heart racing, uncertain of who awaited her on the other side of the door. She opened the door with quite a fear.

To her surprise, it was Mrs. Sheela. She smiled at Shradhha; one could sense a genuity in her smile for the first time.

"Mrs. Sheela, everything okay?" shraddha asked. "Shradhha, I came running to you to tell you that Maya wants to see you; the moment she opened her eyes, you were the first person she asked about... You know what this means... that you did exceptionally well with her... She trusts you, Shraddha." Sheela exclaimed in happiness.

Shradhha was feeling a mixed emotion at that point; she didn't know how to react. Yes, she was happy that Maya trusted her, but she wasn't sure how to face her after that incident during dinner. What if Maya had changed her mind? What if she was upset...?"

She forced a small smile, trying to keep her voice steady. "That's... that's good to hear," she managed to say. "I'm just not certain what to say..."

Mrs. Sheela's smile softened even more as if she understood, "Just be there for her, Shraddha. That's all she needs." She tapped on her shoulder, her touch warm and steady. Shraddha nodded her head.

Shraddha went back to her room, she looked at herself in the mirror, "You should be proud of yourself at least once Shraddha". She whispered, barely audible, as if trying to convince herself.

She put herself together on the way to the hospital, Mrs Sheela accompanied her. Her palms were sweaty as she walked down the hospital corridor. The familiar scent of antiseptic hung in the air, mixing with the low noise of machines and the occasional conversation of nurses. She had been to this part of the hospital plenty of times, but today felt different...like every step was heavier, weighed down by everything she couldn't quite put into words. She took a long breath.

She stopped outside Maya's room, her heart pounding in her chest. She looked at Mrs. Sheela, who smiled, and whispered, "Go". Through the small window, shraddha could see Maya lying on the bed, half-buried under a thin brown blanket. Soft rays of sunlight peeked through the blinds, casting gentle patterns on the wall. Maya's eyes were closed and her head turned towards the window as if searching for something out there.

Shraddha hesitated, then took a breath and knocked lightly before pushing the door open. The gentle creak made Maya move... her eyes slowly opening and finding Shraddha. For a few seconds, they just looked at each other, Shraddha struggling to find the right words, and Maya, blinked, trying to hold back the emotions flooding up in her eyes.

"Hey..." Shraddha said softly, her voice barely more than a whisper.

Maya's lips curved into a small, tired smile as she tried to push herself up, shrinking a bit, "You... you came..."

"Of course I did," Shraddha replied, moving to the chair by the bed and sitting down. "Mrs. Sheela said you wanted to see me."

Maya's eyes were red like she had been crying, but she was holding it together, "I was... I was scared you wouldn't come... after... after that night."

Shraddha's chest stiffened. "No, Maya, I... I am sorry if I made you feel like that, but I'm here, okay? I am not going anywhere." She reached out and held Maya's hand, feeling how cold it was. "I am here for you."

Maya's fingers squeezed hers, a little too tightly, as her eyes flickered with those unshed tears. "Thank you!" she said, her voice breaking. "I... I didn't want to be alone...I was feeling scared."

"You are not alone," Shraddha said, her throat shrinking, "Not anymore."

They just sat there in silence, hands grasped, letting the quiet speak for them. Shraddha knew it would not be easy, but at that moment, she decided that whatever came next, she would be there for Maya, no matter how hard it got.

Over few days, they had settled into a comforting routine, Maya was feeling even better in the presence of Shraddha. Despite the closeness they shared, she made a conscious effort not to press Maya about the decision that had led her to the hospital. She sensed that Maya needed time... time to process, to heal, and to find her own words when she was ready. The last thing she wanted was to make her friend feel confronted or overwhelmed by the weight of her choices.

Maya was discharged from the hospital and came back to Ashraya after a few days.

"Feels good to be back, huh?" Shraddha said, looking over at Maya, who was settling in. Maya nodded, a faint smile tugging at her lips. "Yeah... It does."

It was an unusually warm afternoon, and both of them grabbed seats at their favourite spot, the garden of Ashraya. They sipped tea while looking at the newly grown flowers in the garden which they missed.

Shraddha looked at Maya out of the corner of her eye watching as she gently touched her fingers over the petals of a marigold that had just begun to open. It was a small...simple gesture but filled Shraddha with a quiet sense of relief. It felt like after ages, Maya's smile felt a little less forced, her eyes a little brighter.

"I missed this," Maya said, her eyes fixed on the flowers. "Just sitting here... feeling normal."

Shraddha agreed to her by nodding her head, "Yeah, me too."

"Maya" Shraddha began slowly, glancing at her, "Can I ask you something?? You don't have to answer if you don't feel like it..."

Maya looked at her, slightly hesitant but nodded. "Yes...what is it?"

Shraddha paused, choosing her words carefully, but her voice was steady. "I just... I've been wondering. That night, when everything happened... what made you feel like it was the only way?"

Maya's hand froze, her eyes darkening as she set her cup down. The question felt heavy, and Shraddha suddenly wondered if she'd overstepped. Maya knotted her fingers tightly and whispered, "I...I don't know," she murmured, looking away. It's like...everything felt hollow like there was nothing left in me to keep going. I couldn't see a reason...any reason at all."

Shradhha immediately held her hands, "I can't imagine how heavy that must have felt," she said softly. "I didn't mean to hurt you with my question".

Maya shook her head, her lips pressed in a thin line, as she pulled her hand away, wrapping her arms around herself. "Some things, they're just too hard to explain," she said, her voice heavy.

"Sometimes, Shraddha," she began, her voice terrified, "sometimes, it just feels like everything is closing in, like you're screaming inside, but no one can hear. You... you just want it to stop."

"It's...it's not easy to talk about," Maya began, her words hesitant but determined. "But maybe, just maybe...I'd like to try." Her voice trembled, and she looked away, her eyes become clouded slightly.

Shraddha reached out, her hand resting over Maya's shoulder, steady and warm. "I'll be here," she murmured, her voice steady. "Whenever you're ready, I'll be right here."

They sat together as the sun sank lower in the sky, its warm glow radiating a gentle light around them a quiet promise of hope amidst the shadows.

CHAPTER FIVE

SHATTERED

As Maya spoke, her look softened, and a distant smile appeared on her lips, as if she could almost feel the warmth of those early days.

"I grew up in this supportive neighborhood," she began, her voice gentle. "Everyone knew each other, you know? Kids playing till the streetlights came on, parents calling us in for dinner...it was a nice place to grow up". Her eyes grew warmer with the memory.

"And then, there was Aarav, my best friend.

We met when we were so little, just five, I think. There was this playground not far from where we both lived. That day, I slipped playing hopscotch and scraped my knee. Aarav, who was a stranger then, just a little boy himself ran over and offered me a Band-Aid. He had this serious look on his face, like patching me up was his most important job in the world. After that...we were inseparable."

Shraddha listened carefully, her focus steady as Maya continued, her tone growing lighter with every word.

"We went to the same school, studied together, walked home together. Aarav was... different from my other friends. He was patient and was always there. When I was upset or nervous about something, he would make me laugh and put me at ease without trying too hard. We would talk about everything our wildest dreams, silly secrets, even plans for adventures that seemed so real back then. He was like...my constant, you know?"

Maya paused, her fingers pointing at the edge of her teacup, "Even our parents would remark about how close we were. They used to say that we were like siblings and for me... I guess that's exactly what it was. A bond so natural, so secure, that I trusted him with everything.

She looked at Shraddha, her expression changing, almost like she was bracing herself to move deeper into her story, "To me, Aarav was the one person I believed would never hurt me and someone whom I trusted blindly."

A sudden cloud appeared on her face and Shraddha noticed it...the slight tremble in her voice, the way her fingers gripped the cup just a little tighter.

"As we grew older, things...they began to shift, almost gradually. At first, it was not that noticeable, just tiny moments that I brushed off as normal. Aarav began to pull away at times, but then he would return, almost with more intensity. It would be these moments when we were together, such as sitting in the park or studying at the library, and I would catch him looking at me. But it was...different. His look remained a bit too long, and held something I could not quite comprehend. I would look away, awkwardly laugh it off, thinking maybe I was imagining it."

Shraddha listened to the sadness behind Maya's smile as she recounted these memories.

One evening, we were walking home from school, discussing nothing particularly. He was quiet that day...quieter than usual. When we reached my gate I thought he would just say goodbye and leave. Instead...he turned to me and there was this...intensity in his eyes which I had never seen before. I will never forget it. He took a deep breath and said he had something important to tell me."

Shraddha nodded, sensing how important that moment must have been. Maya's voice grew stronger, though mixed with disbelief.

"He told me he loved me. Not as a friend or as a sister...but really loved me. He said he had felt this way for a long time and that even though he had tried to push it away, he couldn't keep pretending. There was this extreme anxiety in his voice like he was finally letting out something he had held in for so long. And...I was speechless. Aarav had always been my safe space, my constant. I never saw him that way."

"What did you say?" Shraddha asked gently.

Maya sighed, the weight of that memory hanging between them.

"I didn't want to hurt him. I tried to be gentle to let him know that I loved him too but as my friend...as my very own brother. I told him I could not see us any other way. I thought he understood. He smiled, said that he respected my decision and that he was glad to have at least told me. He even joked about us being 'back to normal' the next day. And I believed him, Shraddha. I thought it was all okay. I thought... we'd just go back to being us."

Maya's expression was darkened and her eyes shifted.

"Looking back now, there was a shadow there...a darkness I didn't notice. Or maybe I just didn't want to see it."

"After he confessed his feelings, a few weeks passed, and it felt like things were somehow better. Aarav was more attentive than ever supportive even encouraging me in everything I did. It seemed like he was making an extra effort to show me he valued our friendship. I felt so relieved. I thought I hadn't lost him, that we'd found our balance again."

Shraddha listened attentively, feeling Maya's hurt with every word.

"One evening, Aarav texted, saying he wanted to surprise me with a get together at his home. He didn't say much only that, but just where we could just talk and have fun with our friends without any interruptions. And... I didn't even think to question it. After all, he was Aarav the one person I thought I could trust more than anyone else in the world. I didn't know what lay beneath that familiar smile."

Shraddha held Maya's look, sensing the explosion of emotions brewing within her.

"When I got there, everything seemed fine. There was music playing, a few people talking, but it was quieter than I'd expected, more isolated. I noticed a few unfamiliar faces, but Aarav... he was the one I focused on. He was my friend. I trusted him. I went towards him and asked, "Hey, where is everyone??", but he just smiled, saying they'd left us to catch up. It felt... strange. Something in his eyes wasn't right. Before I could make sense of it, he came closer, blocking my way. His smile vanished, replaced by this cold expression I didn't recognize. I tried to laugh it off, to ease the tension, but he grabbed my wrist...tight, so tight it hurt. I tried to pull back, asked him what he was doing. And that's when he... he showed me the side I had never seen, or maybe never wanted to see."

Shraddha's breath caught, feeling the depth of Maya's hurt and anger.

Maya took a shaky breath, her fingers curling into her palms as she struggled to continue. Shraddha sensed her pain, feeling each word hang in the air, heavy and sore.

"When he first pinned me against the wall, I froze," Maya's voice trembled, her eyes fixed somewhere beyond the present. "For a second, I couldn't process what was happening. This was Aarav, the same Aarav who once wiped my tears when I fell, who cheered me up on my worst days. But there was no trace of him in the eyes that stared back at me. They were cold, filled with something twisted, like I was an enemy he wanted to conquer."

She took a shuddering breath, her hands tightening as if she could still feel his grip. "When I tried to push him away, he grabbed my arms, digging his nails in so hard I felt like he was trying to mark me, like he wanted to show me that I belonged to him somehow and when I said 'no'...it only seemed to fuel his anger. He slapped me, hard, and everything turned for a second. The slap was not just physical it felt like he was wiping out all the years of trust between us."

Her voice dropped, almost to a whisper. "He started saying these awful things...things that distorted every single memory we had shared. He told me that I had led him on, that I had 'made him this way,' that I had taunted him by being close, by confiding in him. Every moment of kindness I had ever shown him...he turned it into something ugly, something that was my fault. And when I tried to reason with him, he just laughed this hollow, mocking sound that shattered whatever hope I had left."

Shraddha's eyes filled with tears, but she stayed silent, letting Maya continue.

"I tried everything...I begged him, I fought as hard as I could, but he was stronger. Every time I struggled, he would just press harder, like he wanted to show me how powerless I was. He leaned in close, his breath hot against my skin, whispering that he would make me pay for rejecting him, that he would make me understand what he felt." Her voice broke, and she looked down, her shoulders shaking. "In that moment... I felt myself shattering. It was like he was taking away every part of me, every bit of my trust, my security. And I could do nothing to stop it."

Shraddha reached out, but Maya pulled her hands close, hugging herself as if trying to hold her broken self together. Her eyes, brimming with tears, met Shraddha's. "After he was done, he just left, as if I were nothing to him. All those years of friendship, of shared memories and laughter...he walked away from it all. And I was left there, broken, questioning everything I'd ever believed about friendship, trust...and myself."

A tear slid down Maya's cheek, though she seemed almost unaware of it. "That night...he took everything from me, Shraddha. My safety, my faith, even my own sense of self. I don't know how to get it back."

te fingers shaking as she recalled, "I couldn't look in the mirror without feeling disgusted. I blamed myself, Shraddha...For being blind to his feelings, for trusting him. Everyone around me kept asking why I'd changed, and I had no words to explain. I couldn't speak, couldn't express the burden I carried."

Shraddha, sensing the weight of Maya's confession, gently asked, "Did you try talking to anyone about what happened?"

Maya's eyes turned dead; her voice soft but laden with a depth of sorrow that seemed to echo from within her.

"When I told people...my friends, those I thought would stand by me...they didn't believe me, Shraddha. It was like screaming into a void. Every word, every plea, was swallowed up, dismissed." Maya's voice cracked, and she gripped the teacup as though it were anchoring her to reality. "They looked at me like I was...like I was the one at fault. I remember going to one of my friends," Maya continued, a bitter edge creeping into her tone. "I barely even got the words out. I didn't even tell her everything... just enough, hoping she'd understand. But her face, Shraddha...she looked at me like I was lying...like some kind...of a stranger." Maya's eyes burned with unshed tears. "She told me maybe I 'misinterpreted' things. That maybe it wasn't what I thought. But I knew. I *knew* exactly what he had done, what he had taken from me."

The silence lay between them, heavy and raw. Shraddha felt a pang in her chest as she imagined Maya standing there, surrounded by friends who had become strangers, doubting her, leaving her alone in her misery.

"I thought my parents would believe me," Maya whispered, her voice barely audible. "But when I finally tried to tell them my words just...dried up. I was scared. Scared they would look at me the same way, scared they would say something that would break me completely. So, I swallowed it all. I kept it in, locking it so deep that even I couldn't feel anything anymore. I just...shut down."

Shraddha clenched her hands, struggling to hold back her tears. "And that's when you...?"

Maya nodded, her eyes drifting to the faint scars on her wrists. "The pain...it felt like it was eating me from the inside out. There were nights when I felt like I was suffocating...like I was drowning in this darkness that no one else could see. I started...hurting myself." She outlined the scars absentmindedly, her fingers trembling. "It was the only way I could feel something that wasn't shame, which wasn't betrayal. For those few moments, I could control the pain...instead of it controlling me."

Shraddha's heart broke at Maya's agony, the weight of her suffering filling the room like an overpowering fog.

"My parents thought I was just being rebellious, that it was a phase," Maya continued, her voice mixed with bitter resignation. "They would try to cheer me up, push me to 'get over it,' without ever knowing what they were asking me to forget." Her lip quivered, and she clenched her fists as if trying to hold herself together. "They didn't see the broken girl hiding inside, the girl who was crying out for help and I would not blame them for that".

Her voice dropped to a whisper, and Shraddha could see tears finally spilling down Maya's cheeks. "I remember one night, I just... I couldn't take it anymore. I was ready to end it. The loneliness, the pain, the emptiness—it all felt too much. I thought, maybe if I could just...disappear, it would all finally stop."

Shraddha's breath caught, a single tear slipping down her cheek.

"But my mother..." Maya's voice shook, her eyes fixed on the scars. "She walked in, just as I was ready to make that final cut. I will never forget the look in her eyes...horror, confusion, but mostly pain. And somehow...seeing her pain pushed me out of mine. I could not go through with it, not after seeing what it did to her."

Maya drew in a shaky breath, her voice thick with emotion. "They took me to a therapist after that, hoping she could fix me like I was some broken doll that they could glue back together. But I could not speak. I could not tell her what had broken me in the first place."

She looked up, her eyes meeting Shraddha's with a spark of something that looked like hope but felt more like surrender. "It was the therapist who told me about Ashraya. She said it was a place where I could finally...breathe. I did not believe her, not at first. But I had nothing left to lose. Nothing."

Shraddha reached out, wrapping Maya's hand with her own. "Maya, you are not alone here. You are safe, and you are not invisible anymore. Whatever Aarav took from you, he cannot take your strength. We are here with you."

Maya's tears flowed freely now, each one washing away a fragment of the pain she had held so tightly. For the first time in years, she felt a small, fragile sense of peace as she allowed herself to be seen, fully and unapologetically... by someone who truly understood.

CHAPTER SIX

WHISPERS

They sat silently for a while, the peacefulness of the Ashraya garden wrapping around them like a gentle embrace. Birds chirped in the distance, and the soft rustle of leaves created a serene backdrop, allowing both women to reflect on their shared yet individual journeys.

Breaking the silence, Maya turned to Shraddha, her eyes filled with curiosity and empathy.

"You have been so strong for me, Shraddha," she begins, her voice soft but steady. "I can't help but wonder...what about you? Have you ever faced something like this?"

Shraddha's gaze falls, her hand gripping the edge of the bench. She feels the weight of her memories pressing down, but as she looks up at Maya, she realizes the significance of this moment...two women, bound by pain, seeking relief.

"I have," Shraddha says quietly, her voice thick with emotion. "It happened a long time ago, during the holidays. I was just a little girl, trusting and naïve. I thought my world was safe."

She pauses, a distant look in her eyes, but she forces herself back to the present, back to Maya. "It was someone I looked up to, someone who should have been a protector."

Maya shifts closer, sensing the vulnerability in Shraddha's tone, and reaches out to hold her hand.

"I...I know that feeling. It is like the world shifts, becomes something you don't recognize anymore," Maya responds, her voice filled with understanding.

A silence settles between them, heavy with shared understanding. Then Shraddha takes a deep breath, obtaining strength from Maya's touch.

"Coming here, to Ashraya...it saved me. I began to realize that healing does not mean forgetting or erasing the past. It means living with it, letting it shape you without letting it control you."

Maya looks at her, admiration softening her features.

"Do you think... that one day I can feel that way too?" Maya asks, her voice mixed with hope.

"Yes, Maya. One day, you will find that peace. But it is not a destination. It is a journey we walk together, step by step," Shraddha replies with a soft smile, a tear escaping down her cheek.

The sun filters through the leaves, casting a warm glow over them as if nature itself is bearing witness to this moment of shared healing.

Maya squeezed Shraddha's hand, drawing comfort from their connection. "Thank you for sharing that with me. It makes me feel less alone in this," she whispered, her voice breaking slightly.

"Always, Maya," Shraddha replied, her heart swelling with hope. "You're not alone. We're in this together."

CHAPTER SEVEN

RESURGE

Later that evening, after Maya had gone to her room, Shraddha found herself in the quiet of her small, personal space. Usually, her room felt like a sanctuary...a place where she could escape and let her guard down. But tonight, the familiar warmth of the space felt heavy, almost stifling, as the words she'd spoken to Maya replayed in her mind. "We're in this together," she had said. Yet here she was, struggling to believe in her own words.

Feeling restless, Shraddha rose from the bed and wandered to the corner of her room. There, on a low shelf, sat the small wooden box...plain, unassuming, but holding memories she hadn't touched in years. This box had travelled with her, tucked away in every place she'd stayed since leaving home. She'd never truly unpacked it, never dared to fully confront what lay inside. But tonight, something drew her to it, an invisible pull she couldn't resist.

Slowly, she lifted the box from the shelf and carried it to her bed, her hands trembling as she placed it on the bedspread. For a moment, she simply stared at it, her fingers hovering over the lid. Taking a deep breath, she opened the box, peeling back the folds of tissue paper with care. The first thing her eyes fell upon was a photograph...a photograph she hadn't seen in years.

It was of herself at eight years old, her hair tied in neat braids, her eyes full of innocence, and her face lit up with the unguarded joy of childhood. She was wearing her favourite red dress. It had been a gift that Christmas, a dress she had loved with the passion only a child could feel. She remembered running through the house that day, twirling and laughing, the fabric swishing around her as she felt like a princess. For a moment, she let herself recall the feeling of pure happiness, the sense that she was safe, that the world was kind, but...after that night, the red dress which was supposed to be a symbol of her childhood joy had become a painful reminder of all that had been taken from her.

Her hands shook as she held the photo, her breath catching in her throat. How could something so innocent hold so much pain? She clenched the photo, feeling her knuckles turn white. The pain felt fresh, raw, as though no time had passed at all.

But then, she remembered Maya; broken and searching for hope, just as she had once been. She had told Maya they were on this journey together, that healing was something they could work toward side by side. Yet here she was, still haunted by the past, still wondering if she could truly help someone else when her own wounds were so deep.

Then another thought struck her, a quieter one that seemed to rise from somewhere deep within. Maybe this was why Mrs. Sheela had asked her to help Maya. Not because she had all the answers, but because she understood the silence, the shame, and the isolation that came with this kind of pain. Maybe she could offer something to Maya simply by standing beside her, even in her own imperfect, wounded way.

As she gazed at the photo, Shraddha felt a flicker of something she hadn't felt in years...resilience. She realized she didn't need to be completely healed to help Maya. She didn't need to erase the pain or forget the past. She simply needed to hold her own story with a little more compassion, to recognize that the strength she had found to survive was the very strength she could share.

Carefully, she placed the photo back in the box and closed the lid, feeling a strange light settle over her. Her past hadn't vanished, nor had the pain disappeared, but it didn't feel as suffocating. She took a steadying breath, a small but powerful affirmation of her own resilience.

A soft knock at the door startled her, and she quickly wiped her damp cheeks, pulling herself together. "Come in," she called, expecting to see one of the other inmates.

The door opened, and Mrs. Sheela stepped in, her usual calm presence filling the room. She took one look at Shraddha's face, and her expression softened with quiet understanding.

"Shraddha," she said gently, "I was taking my usual rounds, then I thought to check on you...I hope that's okay..."

Shraddha felt her throat tighten, overwhelmed by an unexpected surge of gratitude toward this woman who had nudged her, even pushed her, into a role she hadn't thought she could handle. Mrs. Sheela had seen something in her...a strength, a resilience that Shraddha herself had buried under years of silence. By asking her to be there for Maya, Mrs. Sheela had unknowingly opened a path for Shraddha's own healing to begin.

Without thinking, Shraddha crossed the room and wrapped her arms around Mrs. Sheela in a rare, spontaneous hug. She felt the warmth of Mrs. Sheela's embrace, steady and solid, and for the first time, she allowed herself to lean into it. Her heart swelled with gratitude...gratitude for the chance to help Maya and gratitude for the gentle guidance Mrs. Sheela had provided, however unorthodox it might have felt at first.

Mrs. Sheela, surprised but clearly touched, patted her back with a soft smile. "Well now," she murmured, a hint of amusement in her voice. "I don't usually get this kind of response from my residents."

Shraddha pulled back, feeling a little self-conscious but too relieved to care. "Thank you," she whispered, her voice filled with emotion she hadn't allowed herself to express in years. "Thank you for asking me to help Maya. I didn't realize it, but... it's helping me too."

Mrs. Sheela nodded, her eyes warm and knowing. "Healing is rarely a straight path, Shraddha. Sometimes, it's found in the places we least expect."

With that, she gave Shraddha's shoulder a gentle squeeze before stepping back toward the door. As she left, Shraddha felt an unfamiliar sense of hope settling within her. She knew that healing would be a long journey, and there would still be hard days ahead. But she wasn't facing them alone. And now, for the first time, she felt grateful for the presence of others on this path with her.

CHAPTER EIGHT

EMERGE

The sun was dipping lower, casting a warm, golden glow through the windows of Ashraya, filling the hallway with soft hues of amber and honey. As Shraddha made her way down the corridor, her thoughts lingered on Maya's recent smiles...small, hesitant, but real. It was as if a fragile bridge was being built between them, one that took shape slowly, yet felt strong in its own quiet way.

But it wasn't just Maya who seemed to be transforming. Shraddha felt an unmistakable shift within herself. Since that heartfelt talk with Mrs. Sheela, a new sense of purpose had begun to emerge. Each day, she found herself more attuned to the people around her, noticing small details, like the nervous glances from Meena, one of the newer residents, as she prepared the dining area.

Seeing Meena struggle with the plates, Shraddha felt a gentle urge to step in. She crossed the room with soft steps, reaching out to ease Meena's fumbling hands.

"Here, let me help," she murmured, arranging a few plates alongside Meena's, her touch steady and reassuring.

Surprised, Meena looked up, her eyes reflecting gratitude mixed with relief. "Thank you, Shraddha," she whispered. "I get so anxious every time... like I'll mess something up."

Shraddha gave a comforting smile. "You're not doing anything wrong, Meena. We're all here to help each other, remember?" Her voice was a steady anchor, a reminder that none of them had to carry their fears alone.

They finished setting the table in silence, working side by side as the glow of dusk softened the lines of the room. As Shraddha placed the last plate, a quiet warmth blossomed within her, spreading like a gentle balm over old scars. It was the same warmth she felt when Maya looked at her with trust—an affirmation that by lifting others, she, too, was rising.

In that moment, Shraddha realized that healing wasn't just about facing her own pain. It was also about reaching out, even in small ways, to help others with theirs. Each act of kindness, every word of reassurance, was like a stitch in the fabric of her own heart, mending the broken places she had once thought would remain forever torn.

As she glanced around the room, her eyes softened, and she felt a sense of belonging...a quiet, rooted feeling she had almost forgotten was possible. Ashraya was no longer just a shelter; it was a space of shared resilience, a sanctuary where healing happened, one small gesture at a time.

As the dinner began to wind down, Shraddha found herself lingering by the table, watching as the residents continued their quiet evening routines. Each woman moved with her own mix of caution and resilience, and Shraddha felt a quiet pride in simply being part of this space. Across the room, she noticed Meena laughing with another resident, her earlier anxiety softened into something lighter.

Lost in thought, she didn't hear Mrs. Sheela approach until a gentle hand rested on her shoulder. Startled,

Shraddha looked up to see Mrs. Sheela's calm, knowing gaze. There was something in her eyes, a deep understanding, maybe even gratitude...that spoke volumes.

"Thank you, Shraddha," Mrs. Sheela said quietly, her voice warm. "You're helping them more than you realize."

For a moment, Shraddha felt a well of emotions rise within her, a mixture of gratitude and a hesitant joy that felt both foreign and freeing. She didn't say anything, simply took Mrs. Sheela's hand, holding it gently as she looked up, a soft smile on her lips, a quiet acknowledgment of the unexpected path they had both found.

As they stood in companionable silence, Shraddha's eyes drifted to Maya across the room. To her surprise, she saw Maya offering a hand to another resident struggling to carry some cups to the kitchen. There was a look of concentration on Maya's face, but also a faint hint of pride as she balanced the cups carefully. Shraddha and Mrs. Sheela exchanged a glance, a shared, silent understanding.

In that moment, Shraddha felt something solidify within her...a realization that healing often came in the small, steady acts of kindness, of simply being there. She squeezed Mrs. Sheela's hand once more before letting go, the warmth lingering as they both watched Maya take her own first steps toward helping others, a testament to the quiet strength building in each of them.

CHAPTER NINE

RISE

The days had passed in a steady rhythm, each one blending into the next. The light that filtered through Ashraya's windows had changed over the months, growing softer in the mornings, warmer in the afternoons, and deeper in the evenings. Time seemed to flow unnoticed, yet, within Shraddha, things were shifting in ways she had never anticipated.

In the early days at Ashraya, she had been unsure, lost in her own struggles, unsure of her place. But now, months later, there was a quiet steadiness about her. She was no longer the woman who hid from her own reflection, afraid of her scars. Instead, she had learned to wear them like a badge of honour, a testament to her resilience. She had learned to listen, to care, and to give without draining herself. Each day at Ashraya, she found herself more engaged, not just with the women around her, but with her own healing process.

There were moments of doubt, of course, moments when the shadows of her past tried to creep back in. But each time, she had learned to push them aside, finding solace in the simple, everyday acts of kindness. It was in these moments that Shraddha found herself, not in grand gestures, but in the small, quiet acts of love that stitched her heart back together.

It was a quiet Tuesday afternoon when the call came. Shraddha was walking through the hallway, her hands tucked into her pockets, thinking about the evening plans. She had been in a good mood, her confidence slowly becoming a part of her. She was more comfortable now, navigating the halls of Ashraya, greeting the residents, sharing smiles. Life here felt like a steady rhythm, one she had finally come to understand.

Then suddenly, the voice of Mrs. Sheela rang out from behind her.

"Shraddha, could you come to my office for a moment?"

A small jolt ran through Shraddha's chest at the sound of the familiar request, but this time, instead of feeling anxious or fearful, she felt a strange sense of calm. She had been here before, but now she felt different. She was different.

She gave a small nod to Mrs. Sheela and walked confidently towards the office. The door creaked open, and she found Mrs. Sheela sitting behind her desk, her usual poised demeanour softened with a slight, welcoming smile.

"Please, sit down," Mrs. Sheela said warmly, gesturing to the chair in front of her.

Shraddha sat, her posture open and steady, her heart not racing like it once had. She no longer felt the familiar, paralyzing fear that had gripped her in the early days. She was ready to listen.

"Over the past few months," Mrs. Sheela began, her voice carrying a weight of sincerity that made Shraddha's heart flutter slightly, "I've been watching you closely. I've seen you grow. You came to us uncertain, unsure of your place here. But now, I see something different. I see a woman who has found her voice. A woman who has learned not only to give to others but to give to herself, to accept the love and strength that she, too, deserves."

Shraddha looked up, startled by the depth of Mrs. Sheela's words. She hadn't thought about her journey like that before...how, in her efforts to help others, she had quietly begun to heal herself. The thought hit her like a wave, overwhelming and tender at the same time.

Mrs. Sheela continued, her eyes softening. "You have touched the lives of so many women here, Shraddha. Your kindness, your patience, and your willingness to be there for others...it has not gone unnoticed. You've become a source of light in this place. You have helped them find their strength, but more than that, you have found yours."

Shraddha swallowed hard, fighting the surge of emotion rising in her chest. She had never allowed herself to feel proud of what she had done, never allowed herself to see her own transformation. But now, as Mrs. Sheela said, it felt like everything she had done had been leading to this moment, a quiet recognition of her own worth.

Mrs. Sheela leaned forward, her gaze steady. "The team here at Ashraya has noticed what you have done. They want to officially recognize your work. You have become not just someone who helps, Shraddha... you have become an inspiration. You have shown them what true strength looks like."

The words sank in, and Shraddha felt something she had never experienced before, an almost overwhelming sense of pride. Tears pricked at the corners of her eyes, not from sadness, but from something deeper, something more profound. Recognition. Not from her own expectations, but from those around her. She hadn't been looking for it, hadn't even thought that she deserved it. But hearing Mrs.

Sheela say it, with such warmth and admiration, made it feel like she had truly earned it.

"I never thought... I never imagined that I could make a difference like this," Shraddha said, her voice thick with emotion. "I just... I just wanted to help. I didn't realize that I, too, was healing in the process."

Mrs. Sheela smiled a soft, proud smile. "That's the beauty of it, Shraddha. Healing isn't a linear path. It's about learning to give and receive, about accepting the love and strength you so freely give to others. You've done that. And that, my dear, is true empowerment."

Shraddha sat there in silence for a moment, letting the words wash over her, feeling the weight of them settle deep inside her heart. She had spent so long running from her past, so long thinking that she wasn't worthy of love or recognition. But now, she understood, healing didn't just come from fixing others. It came from accepting the grace to heal herself.

"I'm so proud of you, Shraddha," Mrs. Sheela said, her voice quiet but filled with emotion. "And I know the women here are, too. You've shown them that no matter how broken we may feel, there's always a chance for us to rise, to be whole again."

Tears welled in Shraddha's eyes, but this time, they weren't tears of fear or sadness. They were tears of release, of understanding. For the first time in years, she truly felt seen. Truly felt worthy.

As she left Mrs. Sheela's office, Shraddha paused in the hallway, letting the weight of the moment settle in her chest. Recognition had never been the point. The point had always been the quiet realization that she had the strength to face her own darkness, to help others do the same. And now, she realized, she was no longer the broken woman who had walked into Ashraya all those months ago. She was strong. She was whole. And most importantly, she was worthy of love, respect, and a future that was hers to build.

CHAPTER TEN

LIBERATION

As Shraddha sat by the window in the quiet corner of the living room, her thoughts drifted back to the first day she had arrived...nervous, broken, full of doubts. She remembered her sleepless nights, her internal struggles, and how she had buried herself in helping others, all the while too afraid to face her own demons.

But now, it was different. She had faced those fears. She had let the healing happen slowly, in its own time, piece by piece. And in the process, she had helped heal others. In a way, they had all healed together. Each of the women who had come through Ashraya's doors had touched her in ways she could never have imagined.

Her thoughts were interrupted by the soft footsteps approaching from behind. Turning, she saw Maya walking toward her, now standing tall, her posture no longer hesitant or guarded. Shraddha had watched Maya grow in the same way she had grown...each helping the other in a shared journey of recovery. They had learned together that healing was a process, one that didn't happen overnight, but that it was always worth the fight.

"Hey," Maya said softly, standing in front of Shraddha. "You are leaving, aren't you?" Shraddha smiled.

"Yeah," Maya said quietly. "I think it's time for me to move on. But this place...will always be a part of me."

Maya continued...her voice was tight with emotion. "I never would have made it without you. You helped me believe I could be okay again. And now, I'm starting to believe it for real."

Shraddha's eyes softened, and she reached out to take Maya's hand, squeezing it gently. "You're stronger than you think, Maya. You've always had the strength inside you. I'm just glad I was here to help you see it. You deserve every happiness in your life Maya...go seize it"

Maya hugged Shraddha one last time, her embrace filled with silent gratitude before she slowly walked away. Shraddha stood there, her heart full, a tear slipping down her cheek without a word, her smile tender as she let the moment settle in.

As the years passed, Ashraya continued to be a sanctuary for those seeking healing, but Shraddha's journey had come to its own crossroads. She had found peace within herself and discovered that her purpose extended far beyond Ashraya's walls. One afternoon, her parents arrived to visit. Their presence was quiet but reassuring, their understanding evident in their gentle smiles.

"Shraddha," her mother began softly, "It's time, isn't it? You've done so much here, but there's a world outside that needs you too."

Shraddha had always known this moment would come. The thought of leaving Ashraya stirred a bittersweet mix of emotions within her. She had built something here...not just a home, but a family. But she knew her next step would be to take everything she had learned and use it to help even more people.

Her parents had been there through every challenge and victory, quietly waiting for her to be ready to move forward. As Shraddha stood to say goodbye to the place that had shaped her, she knew that she wasn't just leaving Ashraya. She was carrying its legacy forward.

Shraddha's decision to leave was not easy, but it was the right one. She started her own NGO, *Sakhi Foundation*, dedicated to supporting women who had faced trauma. The road was long and full of challenges, but Shraddha was determined. Her foundation offered more than just aid—it offered empowerment, hope, and a way for women to reclaim their lives.

With the support of volunteers and professionals, *Sakhi* grew steadily. What started as a small initiative soon blossomed into a full-fledged organization, touching the lives of countless women. Shraddha's vision had always been clear: to provide a safe space where women could heal, rebuild, and rediscover their strength. And slowly, piece by piece, she saw it coming to life.

The foundation's programs expanded to include counseling, job training, legal advocacy, and mentorship. It became a place where women not only survived but thrived. Shraddha often found herself reflecting on the journey she had taken, from the broken woman who arrived at Ashraya to the woman who now stood at the helm of an organization changing lives.

Years later, Shraddha sat in her office, reviewing the progress of *Sakhi Foundation*. She looked at the many success stories, at the women who had walked through the doors as strangers but had left as empowered individuals. The room was filled with the sound of typing and conversations as staff members worked tirelessly to continue the mission Shraddha had started.

She glanced up as Maya, now a trusted counselor and leader within *Sakhi*, entered the room. Their bond had deepened over the years—both had healed and grown together, and now they were building something far bigger than they had ever imagined.

"Hey," Maya said, smiling warmly. "I was thinking about how far we've come. When you first started this, I don't think either of us realized just how much this place would change lives."

Shraddha looked up from her work, her heart swelling with pride. "We've come a long way, haven't we? And we still have so much more to do. This is just the beginning."

Maya nodded, her eyes gleaming with the same passion Shraddha had once carried. "It is. And I'm glad we're doing this together."

As Shraddha looked at Maya, she felt a deep sense of gratitude for the journey they had shared. She had helped Maya heal, but Maya had also helped Shraddha find the courage to build something lasting. Their shared purpose had created an unbreakable bond between them, one that would continue to empower others for years to come.

Shraddha had come full circle. From Ashraya to *Sakhi Foundation*, her journey had taken her from the depths of pain to the heights of healing. And as long as there were women in need, Shraddha knew she would continue to fight for them, just as she had fought for herself.

As Shraddha stood there, her heart full, she realized that this was no longer just her journey. It was a journey shared by every woman who had walked this path. And together, they would keep moving forward.

"The future was theirs to shape. And Shraddha knew, with all her heart, that this was just the beginning"

"SPREADING HOPE"

"Gather your courage and fly"

A Tribute To Every Woman's Journey

"To all the women who have endured the unimaginable, who have fought silent battles, and to those still struggling to find their way ... your strength is a testament to the power of the human spirit. To those who have lost their lives, your pain is not forgotten, and your memory fuels the fight for justice and healing. For every tear shed, for every step taken, for every scar that tells your story, know that you are loved, you are worthy, and you are not alone. Your courage gives us hope, and your journey inspires us all to rise, heal, and never give up."

The Road Ahead

This book is the culmination of those stories that spoke of pain, resilience, and the quiet yet powerful strength within every woman. To all the women whose journeys I've had the privilege to witness, and whose courage inspired these words, I owe my deepest gratitude. Your experiences, though difficult, serve as a beacon of hope for others walking the same path.

I also want to thank my near and dear ones who supported me throughout the writing process. Your encouragement and belief in me, especially when self-doubt crept in, were the pillars on which I stood. A special note of thanks goes to Lithin Thampy, throughout the editing process showed an incredible understanding of the narrative, allowing the heart of the story to shine while ensuring it remained coherent, engaging, and polished, and to the team at Notion Publishers for their invaluable insight and dedication, which helped bring this book into the world.

Writing this story has been a deeply personal journey...one of healing and rediscovery. It has taught me that the strength to heal doesn't lie in the absence of scars, but in how we choose to wear them. Shraddha and Maya's stories, while fictional, are voices of the many women who have found the courage to rebuild their lives. This journey is never easy, and it is never done alone.

Through the story of Shraddha, I wanted to convey that no matter how broken we may feel, there's always a chance to rise, to heal, and to embrace the power of resiliance.

Though the pages of this book have come to an end, the journey continues....for all of us. In each woman's story lies the seed of hope, and together, we continue to move forward.

As a final thought, let this resonate in your heart:

""Healing isn't about moving on...it's about learning to live again, stronger and more whole than before.""